TALES OF THE
BOY IN
WINTER

Grim stories about horrible people

J R Holden

For my dad, the naughtiest boy in 1942

Tales of the Boy in Winter

Stories and interruptions

CONTENTS

Introduction

my neighbours are driving me insane. Don't take what I say literally. It's the noise they make. I think they're attempting to decorate, but they are removing the wallpaper with a spoon. That's what it sounds like, with all that scraping.

They have a dog, and it barks at all hours. Not good if you're trying to sleep. I told them I should report this to the appropriate authority, but I don't like getting people into trouble. I don't understand what, in my statement, provoked such an angry response. I mean, it's them that are irritating me, not the other way around.

They're not young – the couple next door. I'd say mid-thirties. Jeff and Annette. Jeff is one of these stocky types, with thick eyebrows. Actually, it's more of a monobrow. I always think of werewolves when I see him shambling up the street, especially when he wears that donkey jacket. Annette dyes her hair. She tries talking nicely to me over the fence, but it's when I'm tending to my geraniums. I have said she can come in for a cup of tea, but she hasn't taken up my kind offer, which is a shame, because I could have explained what they need to do differently to be reasonable human beings. I think I could get through to her.

I liked it better when the house next door was empty. Jean lived there, for many years. She left about the same time George went on his walk. I liked Jean.

These new people, though. They're inconsiderate. I've got the radio on now, my favourite Just a Minute. I can't hear Nicholas Parsons for the racket they're making, and the dog's barking again. I'm going to bang my rolling pin on the wall…

You will have to excuse my digression. I wanted to present to you, dear reader, three short stories written by my late mother. I have heard that they are true, if slightly manipulated. Tales handed down through the family. My mother was an author. Perhaps you have heard of '*The Truth behind the Hermit of Warkworth*' or '*Lead Coffin burials in Yorkshire*'? Maybe not, they're out of print now.

There are more. I found them in an old journal in her loft as we cleared her house. George put them straight into our loft, and it's only recently I've been able to get them down to look through. I didn't want to disturb those big fingerprints he'd left on the box, but we have to move on, don't we?

Without further ado, I present to you The Beginning.

I am intrigued as to how it all started. Quite shocking to think these things happened in your family. I mean, my grandfather was a postman, and his brother a manager at the soap mill. You can't get more decent than that.

I believe that my dear mother spiced it up for publication, probably egged on by her publisher, or my brother who has always enjoyed taking risks with other people's money.

While I remember, for those of you whose parents did not educate you about barghests and lycans, I have written a Glossary at the back.

My apologies for rambling. Please read on and make your own mind up about my heritage.

Hannah Miller   June 1974

Ghosts

'Some say they are spirits of the dead, attracted to the light of the living. Do not engage with them. They will fade like old lace.'

Elizabeth

No-one could have predicted the grotesque events that would take place as a consequence of George Cummings marrying the woman of his dreams. Some followed much later, and it could be argued that they were unrelated occurrences, brought about by the follies of those involved, or just bad luck. Nonetheless, for a short time, Mr Cummings of Greald was the most contented he had ever been.

A widower for five years, George Alfred Edward Cummings was, to coin a phrase from the great American philanthropist P. T. Barnum, 'a catch'. Gifted with financial security and of a sound mind, he was of upstanding character and breeding.

Mr Cummings wanted a fine male heir, and Isobel White, recently appointed as his daughter's nanny and governess had a comely face with pale skin and silky dark hair that she always pinned up, with a comb of carved bone. Isobel carried herself with quiet grace and would take well to pious domesticity. And he secretly craved something more than the mundane. A little magic, you might say. This he could see in her.

The ceremony took place in the small village church, and it was in the little walled graveyard where she walked afterward with a tear on her cheek. Her only regret, she told him, was that her parents were not alive to witness the happy occasion, having expired only a few months earlier, in her hometown far away. Not that she had any qualms about her current position. The village of Greald was far from any metropolis, but there was a butcher, baker, fishmonger (on a Friday), and a pond. And everyone had been polite to her when she arrived. What more could she ask for?

He held her close and felt her heart beat fast against his chest. Her cool hand touched his neck, and he knew he would want for nothing else in this world.

Mrs Brown, the butcher's wife, told Mrs Smith, the baker's wife, that Mr Cummings would rue the day he ever set eyes on such a temptress. That woman, Mrs Brown was sure, had been sent to distract the menfolk, and she'd had to dig a distracted Mr Brown in the ribs when Isobel White walked past the shop with her basket of herbs gathered from the fields. There was nearly a chopped finger in the sausage meat that day.

Mrs Smith wondered that Mr Brown's hand did not slip when his wife leant across the counter to admonish him about the generous cuts of meat he gave to his customers. But this was a joyous occasion; everyone was invited up to the big house and given a week's leave on the rent.

The marriage seemed blessed when, two months later it was announced that Isobel was with child.

Mr Cummings was so pleased he had the church bells ring all day, giving poor Miss Hubert, the seamstress with consumption who lived (or rather was in the throes of her last day on earth) next to the church, the added inconvenience of earache.

Mr Cummings glowed with happiness as he walked through the village on the long summer days, out to the field in which sat his lovely Isobel.

However, as her belly grew, Isobel's skin paled and her hair lost its lustre. The doctor at first told Mr Cummings it was part of the natural process, nothing to worry about; but lively Isobel no longer gathered herbs in the field. She sat in her room with the curtains closed, and left the house at dusk, walking down to the little graveyard where her concerned husband would find her red-eyed, wringing her hands. This was not part of the natural process, he knew. His first wife blossomed when she carried his daughter, Elizabeth.

The original Mrs Cummings was a dutiful, industrious lady who had cherished her solo expeditions to the city where she would buy household items, gifts for him—small leather bound prayer books, and cotton caps for her baby girl. She had, unfortunately, expired of a contagious fever caught on a journey to London, when their daughter was not yet weaned from the wet nurse's breast. Fortunately, Mrs Cummings had only taken the coachman on that trip, and he was easily replaced.

The doctor could provide no answer to the puzzle of Isobel's fading illness, despite many examinations, and scouring of his text-books. In frustration Mr Cummings paid a visit to Old Jeannie the village midwife. As her name suggested, she had the advantage of much maturity, as seen in her bright white locks, and deeply wrinkled skin. She had the gnarly cough that comes from too much pipe-smoking, but she was not brittle. Some said she oiled her bones with a sweet-smelling liquid she made herself from water, yeast and honey. Mrs Smith had gained a small amount for her husband's painful condition and was quite surprised to find that, instead of rubbing it into his knees, he was supping it. How repulsive!

Old Jeannie lived in a cottage next to the lake. It was more of a falling down barn. She lived a plain life and, it was rumoured, she'd only ever had two baths in her life. Old Jeannie was wont to give advice that was occasionally wise, but always very clear. Mr Cummings was desperate. He stood in the hovel's doorway, so he could breathe the clear outside air as he listened, and Old Jeannie did not mince her words. She threw some unsavoury items into the pot that hung above her fire and told him he would lose his wife and gain a son. Not the news Mr Cummings wanted to hear. Both exchanged sharp words before he gave her a day's notice on her accommodation and hurried back to his beloved ailing wife.

The birth was difficult and painful. Isobel developed a fever. In her ravings, she mentioned dark shadows in graveyards and bled rather a lot. Mr Cummings paced the hall until the doctor emerged to tell him he had gained a son but lost a wife.

He buried his beautiful dead Isobel under an oak tree in the corner of the little graveyard she had so diligently frequented. Not quite the ending Mrs Brown had envisaged. Mr Cummings had the church bells ring a solemn note all that day and every Sunday after for a whole year.

George Cummings sat in a darkened room in the house, with a painting of his beloved wife and received no visitors. He told Mrs Miskin the housekeeper to keep his little son away from him. He had lost the only person he had truly loved, and this baby was to blame.

Occasionally he allowed his daughter in, to read from the bible, even though it gave him scant comfort.

His daughter Elizabeth had inherited some of his family's finer facial features and her mother's fair curls. In her father's presence she was quiet and demure, this way she gained favour. She might have believed that he couldn't hear her in the parlour screaming and stamping her feet when she wanted something, but he had no time for an inconvenient headache, so he always gave her what she wanted.

With everything she wished for (apart from being a princess) Elizabeth should have been the happiest little girl in the Empire. But a cloud darkened her sunny sky. The baby born of her expired step-mother. What an odious creature it was, lying in its crib like a china doll. It wouldn't even open its eyes when she demanded it.

Everyone said the baby was quiet, but he wasn't when she was there. He screamed like the baby pig she'd held up by its tail in the Tuckett's sty. Fascinating that these small pink animals didn't enjoy being prodded, but she only did it to see how healthy they were.

There was some concern in the household that his mother had passed her fever to him the way he vomited up black fluid. The doctor did much scratching of his chin, and sighing over the crib, to no avail. No-one saw the little girl in the stable early in the morning, gathering mouse droppings in her lace handkerchief to take into the nursery.

Elizabeth called him 'Piglet' until Mrs Miskin told her not to. She didn't know his name, and neither, she was sure, did the housekeeper.

He was put next to her in Church, when he was big enough, but was never there at the end of the service. Mrs Miskin would have to walk across the little graveyard to Elizabeth's step-mother's grave, where the little boy draped himself, to tell him to come home.

Elizabeth couldn't remember when he stopped sitting on the family pew. She missed prodding him when her attention wandered from the sermon. She had to resort to sticking her tongue out at the postman's son who always stared at her when they sang the second hymn.

George Cummings never came to terms with losing his beloved second wife, despite four years later, becoming betrothed to a young woman from a good family in York. Her father, however, did not allow the marriage to take place, as he had concerns, not over the financial status, nor the character of his future son-in-law. It was the time Mr Cummings spent in his study staring at the picture of the pale-skinned, dark-haired second wife.

Undeterred, George Cummings continued his search for a suitable spouse, so it was five years and forty-five days after the lovely Isobel's demise, that he took his third wife. Miss May Springfield, a lady from a nearby town, came from good stock but was a little homely to be 'netted' in her early years.

Miss Springfield liked things simple. She had an overly large King James Bible that was always open on her bureau when her husband-to-be visited. She sniffed at light-hearted sentimentality, practising patience, piety, and industry about her parents' home. She would be an excellent household manager.

When she arrived, Elizabeth was brought to her, with a delightful smile, neat ringlets, and very polite curtsy. So impressed was the new Mrs Cummings by the girl's demeanour that she relinquished one of the three sweetmeats put back for the evening, to consume before climbing into her groom's bed.

The little girl looked up with large blue eyes, and said she was eternally grateful, but couldn't possibly deprive the lovely lady of her treat. This Mrs Cummings was most impressed by such strength of mind from one so young.

'Are there any more like you, dear?' she asked.

'No, madam,' Elizabeth truthfully said. 'Just me.'

As the bride mounted the stairs in the evening, she was caught by a strange sound, carried down from above. In the dim light and dark surroundings, it sounded eerie, and disturbed the new Mrs Cummings. It was like the keening of a wounded feline. But the cat of the house lived in the barn across the courtyard. She had heard of Mr Cummings's misfortune with the second wife, delicate and sickly, and wondered if such a sad soul lingered within the confines of the dull walls. In fact, so distressed was she by the quiet wails, she went straight into her box and ate all the sweetmeats, without pausing for breath.

The very next day she started with the idea conceived whilst she had waited in the gloomy bedroom, for Mr Cummings to come up from the study, where he had been delayed by his work. The dreary old house was 'opened up' with new curtains and handmade carpets imported from Persia (As told by the well-dressed gentleman standing on the dock side in Hull, who had asked a princely sum for his wares, accepted by a weary Mrs Miskin sent on the errand to procure such items. The housekeeper regretted being in such a smelly, busy place, when she craved to be in the Minerva public house with her gin and banana fruit). The fading wallpaper was painted over in a fresh deep red, and the floorboards scrubbed with turpentine and beeswax.

Mr Cummings was a benevolent husband. Mrs May

Cummings had a fine domestic allowance with full financial responsibility for the household (Mrs Miskin continued with the practicalities). She had not had an indulged life prior to her nuptial arrangement and initially blanched at the amount of money this entailed, but swiftly adapted. Her husband, with great faith in his new wife, continued to manage the estate from the study. All was well. Apart from the odd ghostly wail, which Mrs Cummings eventually put down to wind in the pipes.

In the ninth year of the second Mrs Cummings' departure from this world, the stable cat went up to the attic and delivered a litter of kittens under a chair. She wasn't perturbed by the shape on the chair that looked like a pile of old clothing, nor by its occasional noise. A sob. A sigh.

Here was the source of Mrs Cummings' ghostly wailings. A forgotten little spirit cast aside in grief. This cool dark place had become familiar to the boy. He no longer slept in a comfortable bedroom, sat at the table in the dining room, or walked head bowed down the road to the little church.

A bed of blankets near the window, and a nip into the kitchen for scraps sufficed. Most of the time he sat and listened to the sounds of the house during the day; the people talking, doors creaking, Elizabeth laughing.

His world was of shadowy walls, living with the discarded furniture and old books and creeping around with the small creatures that frequented the nooks and crannies. Sometimes he prayed to turn into a mouse. It might not be so hard to take cheese from the kitchen, and water from the well in the courtyard.

Now, something disturbed his musings of misery. Soft and warm, it bounced off his leg as he languished on the chair.

He looked down and saw three multi-coloured mites mewling and rolling around. What strange creatures they were, soft squeaking bodies of fur with large eyes, and wobbly gait. They left their mother and explored, prodding with tiny paws, running trails of prints in the attic dust. As they grew in confidence, they discovered each other, play fighting, rolling around. Three bodies in one big fur ball. They sped across the floor, knocking over vases and old pictures, unaware of the dark eyes that watched. They worked a strange magic, teasing out the strands of his soul with their little claws.

Mrs Miskin, disturbed by the strange sounds, opened the door to investigate, and found a boy standing amongst knocked over pictures and broken vases with three little kittens in his arms. At first she wondered how this repulsively ragged child had got into the house, but as she looked into his face, she saw the eyes of Isobel.

When she admonished him for causing such mayhem, he gazed at her in such a way that she got a feeling in her chest; not a pain as such, more like the warm pressure she got when too close to the fire on an evening. So, she helped him clean up the mess, and told him not to tell anyone about animals in the loft as Mrs Cummings might find out and then there would be 'Hell to pay'. But she was more concerned about how the butcher's and baker's wives might take the revelation of an heir being discovered in the attic, wearing trousers that were far too small.

She took him downstairs, to the kitchen, got out the tin bath, and found some clothes that fitted. He looked more decent, with his hair combed, and a pair of shoes on.

Young Master—what was his name? At least he was tidy now, but in need of some direction with manners… seen as how he ate his cheese.

Mrs Miskin thought she had dealt quite stealthily with the problem; however, she had been discovered.

Young Elizabeth had seen the dirty urchin being taken down the back stairs. She did not present herself for dinner and was nowhere about the house. Mrs Cummings found her lying still on her bed, fingers like ice. Elizabeth tried to tell her step-mother not to bother her father, but he was too busy in his study to answer the knock on the door. Mrs Cummings took matters into her own hands, being very concerned as the little girl has lost her lustre. She called the doctor. He said she had a chill. She only picked up when her step-mother draped her own lace shawl about the girl's shoulders, and propped her by the fire, with a plate of sweetmeats on her lap.

The next morning, when Mrs Miskin went into the boy's room to wake him, the bed was made up, the bowl of water on the side table untouched. The attic was empty and quiet, and so she got on with her duties. There was always work to do, and little time to do it in.

Christmas that year was a joyous time for the blossoming Elizabeth. Her father came briefly out of his study and she showed him her new dress, boots, coat and various coloured ribbons; and the leather-bound Bible which she promised she would look at every night. Indeed, she did. She looked diligently at the shelf on which it lay, before she knelt on the floor near her bed to give thanks for all the gifts she had received; and to ask for more, especially the red shoes she had seen in the shoemaker's shop. And not forgetting to request that the horrible boy who lived in the attic disappeared.

He was most irritating (although not now odoriferous) the way he crept about the place, like… how to describe that shifting shadow? A small resurrectionist. He ate like a pig on the food he stole from the kitchen. Wherever she went, there were crumbs. In the washhouse, the yard, the stable. There were traces of him everywhere. A footstep in the snow. An empty plate in the barn. A Christmas rose on her step-mother's grave. A scattering of soil in the passageway. A labourer's child wearing the boy's hat.

As she walked about his room, looking for something to destroy, she heard a noise in the space above. It sounded like laughter, but it couldn't be. She was the only person who expressed mirth in this house.

Elizabeth went quietly up to the servants' quarters, mindful that she was entering unchartered territories. But it wasn't William, or Mr Rice making such a racket. Peeping into the room full of old furniture, she saw the little boy playing in the dust with the young cats. His face was bright. Full of joy.

A horrible turn overcame her. It made her feel quite sick.

From that day for a very long time she was pale and quiet. When she came out of her room, she sat on her swing in the sunshine, looking up at the small attic window, until it was too dark to see. Mrs Cummings was quite concerned. Her lovely step-daughter's hair lost its shine, and the curls fell out before she had the chance to put the ribbon in. She no longer smiled.

Mrs Cummings called the doctor. He diagnosed malaise and prescribed a tonic.

That night there was a summer storm, and some disturbing noises woke Mrs Cummings. She alerted Mrs Miskin, who awoke old William the butler who then disturbed Mr Rice (junior) the footman. After inspection of the outside, he returned in a damp state, and said the guttering had finally fallen down. Whilst he and young David, the page, battled with a ladder (and the wind), Mrs Cummings went into Elizabeth's room and found a whirlwind inside. The window was smashed. Her doll lay in pieces on the hearth, her trinkets scattered across the rug, and some of her bedclothes hanging from the window.

Elizabeth was in bed, fast asleep, and took some rousing. She asked sweetly if her step-mamma was well when she came to.

The distraught Mrs Cummings could get no reply knocking on her husband's door. He was not in his bedroom; she found him in his study. He was not pleased with the disturbance.   What he was doing there in the small hours, she was unsure of. He had seemed to stare at a picture above the fireplace, before he told her to 'go away and stop bothering me.'

It quite knocked the wind out of her sails, and the next morning she rose with a terrible pain in her head, which only eased when she arrived at her parent's house (she had told her husband three weeks previously that she would have to visit her mother), with her portmanteau and a soggy handkerchief.

She returned a week later, bringing a pair of new red shoes for Elizabeth, which raised some colour to the girl's cheeks.

That same day, the little boy went into the attic to see his furry friends and found their tiny bodies lifeless on the floor. The remains of some strange smelling sweetmeat lay near the window.

He buried them under the tree in the graveyard and lay next to the little mounds until evening when the vicar told him to go home because it was getting very dark, particularly in that corner of the graveyard.

Elizabeth's health improved with the return of her step-mother. She put her new red shoes on the shelf, next to the Bible, so she could look at them every night. She wore them on her birthday when she opened all of her presents, and also when Mrs Cummings took her into the town to have her fitted for a lovely new dress with a pink sash.

She enjoyed the long summer playing with her new dolls; telling Mrs Miskin's young niece to fetch her drinks and cakes from the kitchen. Her pink cheeks filled out, as did her new dress and Mrs Cummings had to get the seamstress in the town to let it out a little.

No-one saw the boy for a long time. Mrs Miskin eventually found him at his mother's graveside, crouched and still like a stone. She thought he was dead; he was so pale. It gave her such a fright when he breathed that she nearly ran back to the house. But seeing that he was ill (and that the vicar had noticed them) she had to take action. He was bigger than when she'd last seen him, and in need of another new pair of trousers. He was cold and unresponsive, so she brought out Mr Rice (junior) who carried him back and put him in his room.

By then it was dinner time, and the family sat at the table, waiting for their food. When Mrs Miskin told Mr Cummings that his son was very ill, the benevolent gentleman sat in silence, staring at his cutlery, hands folded together as if in prayer.

Mrs Cummings rose immediately, with a gasp, displaying knitted eyebrows. She was having difficulty speaking and looked like she had swallowed whole one of the lemon curd tartlets she liked to have for supper.

'Mrs Miskin,' Mr Cummings said. 'Leave now and take my daughter with you.'

As the housekeeper closed the door, she heard Mrs Cummings cough then splutter out: 'What does she mean, George, you have a son?'

The heavy oak, barely concealed the rather heated conversation that took place, mainly the high-pitched tones of Mrs Cummings, demanding to know what was going on, before Mr Cummings told her he didn't have a son, or rather, if nature took its course, he would be taken soon.

Mrs Miskin distracted the young mistress with the suggestion of something sweet whilst she waited for her meal. Off went Elizabeth, fair skipping to the kitchen, her face full of glee.

Mrs Cummings went to see the boy who lay somewhere between the living and the dead. She sniffed and said to Mrs Miskin that it would seem her husband was correct in his calculations, then went to her room, demanding a lemon curd tartlet on her favourite plate, and did not come out until the morning.

There was some talk after church for a few weeks, about Mr Cummings's heir, but most said it wasn't true. Everyone knew Isobel Cummings' baby had died at birth. Fingers pointed to Mrs Miskin making up stories because she was old and senile (Mrs Brown), or lacking her own offspring (Mrs Smith).

There was an unnecessary interruption when little Annie Tuckett, a labourer's daughter, asked if they meant the dark-haired foundling boy who sat at the back, next to her and had given his hat to her ailing brother. She was reminded of the wise saying: 'little girls should be seen and not heard.'

Mrs Miskin had some experience of the world. She'd been to York, and the market at Beverley, and held her own against the wagging tongues. She cast some aspersions about the quality of flour, and lack of flavour in the sausages. No-one got away with saying she was a liar.

The shadows lengthened, and the leaves turned brown on the trees. Wood was gathered for the cold winter ahead. Many of the farmers said this would be a tough one. There had been a poor harvest, and farm labourers shivered next to empty grates.

But Elizabeth shone like a bright star in the Sunday congregation, with her lovely ringlets and red shoes. Mrs Brown told Mrs Smith that the girl would be a heartbreaker. Mrs Smith agreed. Both unaware of the boy that laid in his bed at the Cummings' house, whilst the little ghosts of his furry friends blew across the attic floor, leaving only dust and tears.

Mrs Cummings was pragmatic as December approached. Without a thought of the sick child (whom she believed to have already expired quietly and without fuss, as hoped for), she prepared for the festive season. She was having a pair of red boots made for Elizabeth, from beautiful soft calf skin. There was also a new dress, a cape, pearl necklace for the budding young lady. She commissioned a painting of herself to replace the one in the study above the fireplace. She had also ordered a half dozen of the exotic new fruit called oranges as a special surprise. She was sure she could draw her husband away from his work.

But Elizabeth was not as content as she hoped. The boy remained in the physical realm, according to the parlour maid, still as death, but not yet in that peaceful repose. And the attention lavished upon him! Mrs Miskin took him the best cheese and mutton; and was always changing the sheets, lighting fires, opening windows, then closing them, as with the curtains. The doctor came too, more often than she had ever seen him. Although this stopped when Mrs Miskin received the medical bill.

It irked Elizabeth that she must sleep with only a wall

between them. A thin layer of brick and plaster. Some nights she fancied she could hear his breaths creeping through. Recently she had been plagued with strange thoughts as she stared up at the grey ceiling, listening to the owl call up the moon. She wondered if her late step-mother had been a gypsy, with her dark eyes and hair. The woman still haunted her, even though it had been so long since she took her last breath. She fancied she heard her light footstep in the courtyard outside, as the stars lit her way back from the fields. Had Isobel White already been with child before she had married Elizabeth's father? That would be reason enough for him to shun the boy. Perhaps the father was a drunkard or a beggar? A rat catcher? Or a leech collector?

Such thoughts kept her occupied when shadows were dark, and the air was cold on her face.

In the space above, a mouse ran across the attic floor. Its tiny feet crossed the paths of smudged paw prints, changing, as memories do, when the dust shifts in the air. The mouse paused for a moment, disturbed by a noise. A swish, and a clatter. It tried to run, but something came out of the shadows. Something large…

The little boy sensed it in the room below. He pulled back the blankets, breathing in the cold night air and looked up at the ceiling.

Mrs Miskin heard it in the room next to the attic. At that moment, she was in a paroxysm of anxiety over how to pay the doctor's bill without the Cummings's knowledge. The noise sounded to her like the stick Mr Cummings would beat her with, for even considering raiding the tin he kept locked in the second drawer down in his desk, in the study.

Mrs Cummings heard it as well. 'At least,' she thought, 'it isn't the drainpipe outside the room coming loose.' But she would send Mr Rice (junior) up the ladder at daylight, just to make sure…

Elizabeth didn't hear it. She was sound asleep, dreaming of small cats that ran around her, nicking her shins with their sharp claws.

17

It was an awkward moment, the next evening, when Mr Cummings disturbed his wife's cross stitching in the Drawing Room. He usually carried himself with decorum, and some grace, but not that night. She reacted badly to his somewhat negative comments about brightening up his study with her portrait. She attempted to explain that the other picture, being dowdy, was put away in the attic. Was she not the keeper of his home, endowed with such talents as taste and refinement? Had he not left the job of keeping and caring for the house in her hands?

How was she to know that money was less abundant this year? It was he who made the money. She merely spent it. And not on herself. On every other member of the family, but herself. She'd definitely not taken any money out of the tin he kept in the second drawer down, in his desk, in the study. How dare he accuse her of such thievery? And how ridiculous that he should demand the items she had purchased be returned to their makers immediately. It was past nine in the evening.

She bustled from the room, and at ten entered her husband's study, briefly, with a bulging portmanteau. She was going back to her mother's and would come back in a few days when Mr Cummings's even temper had returned.

Mr Cummings wished her a Merry Christmas, even though this was ten days away, and ensured her safe delivery into the waiting carriage. He then went up into the attic, coming down with a large oblong parcel, which he took into the study, along with a full bottle of brandy.

Mrs Miskin informed Elizabeth the next morning that her step-mother had a fever and was being nursed by her kin.

Elizabeth wasn't daft. She'd heard angry voices the previous evening. Mrs Miskin was giving nothing away, so she took her father's tea tray into the study. He was silent, sitting at his desk, papers around him, staring at the inkwell. Behind him on the wall, Isobel White who had been her nanny for such a short time and step-mother for less, looked down on her. There was something about the eyes that disturbed young Elizabeth. Dark cold depths, she fancied. The Romanies had black eyes, didn't they? They could cast a curse on people who tried to harm them. Such dark magic went beyond the grave, did it not?

Her father sat under those eyes every day.

As she looked at him, she saw how hunched he was. She'd not noticed his large hooked nose before. With a dark day suit on, he looked like a crow, bent over a piece of carrion.

Whilst she was in her room later, the creaking of floorboards above interrupted her dark thoughts. The sound came from the junk room. The boy was in his bed next door, and all the servants were about their duties. So, who was up there?

Her question remained unanswered and continued to perplex her even when she lay in bed at night, as the cold wind rattled the glass, and the drainpipe outside her window moaned like a lost soul…

Mrs Miskin was woken in the early hours by a dishevelled young mistress. Her eyes were all puffy and her face blotched. She was gasping and puffing like an old woman, and said it was horrible, and that Mrs Miskin had to come at once. There were cats running around her room, keeping her awake.

The housekeeper got up, wrapping her shawl around her, silently cursing this spoilt child. She remembered the hot summer, when the sun baked the soil solid, and her little niece ran up and down, out to the swing where Elizabeth sat, waiting for her plates of sweetmeat and special glass of water.

Elizabeth scurried at her side as they walked down the creaking stairs, along the dark corridor to her room.

'My ankles,' said the girl, pointing to her smooth skin. 'Look what they've done. I want them out my room this instant.'

Mrs Miskin looked in the bedroom and saw nothing. Just the girl's Bible on its shelf, her red shoes by the wardrobe, and the night basin on the floor. The girl had brought in mud earlier on her shoes. It was smudged all over the carpet...

This happened the following night. And the one after that, and so on, until poor Mrs Miskin had to put the girl in her own little bed, whilst she slept in a chair, with a thin blanket wrapped around her, breath steaming in the cold air.

But the housekeeper had a weight on her shoulders that kept her eyes open and her mind busy. The boy in bed wasn't improving. Whenever she went in, he was still and quiet under the bedcovers. The mistress remained at her mother's. Tradespeople kept turning up at the door with brown parcels, holding out their hands for payment. The roof in old William's room had started leaking. And to top it all Mr Cummings was smelling more like her late husband Bert, when he used to come back from The Broken Barrel, a drinking establishment of ill repute in the nearby town.

On the eve of Christmas, the Tucketts and Johnsons came calling. The poor of the area had a habit of visiting their employers at this time of year, requesting money but not offering any service for it.

Unfortunately, Mrs Miskin was at her sister's after the woman had taken a turn, cook had the night off, Mr Rice (junior) was in the barn with the parlour maid (showing her how to tie a bale of hay), David the page had been sent home to his family and old William had tumbled off the ladder whilst inspecting the gutter. Mr Cummings was still at work in the study. It fell upon Elizabeth to answer the door.

She looked out at the people gathered in the dark.

'Little mistress, do you have something for us?' Mrs Tuckett came forward. 'Keep us going through the winter.'

Her father opened the study door and issued his usual response to parcel deliverers.

'What's that? There's no money. Go away!'

The children cried when she repeated her father's words. They were small, like her half-brother, and odious. One of them wore a familiar hat. It hurt her chest to look at it. He cried more when she took it and threw it on the stairs.

They smelled like chicken manure, and she wanted them away from the door.

Mr Tuckett, despite this strange reaction, remained reasonable. 'All we're wanting is firewood,' he said. 'If you've got any to spare, we can go home and boil our potatoes.'

He was gaunt, as they all were. The Tucketts and Johnsons. Hunger darkened his eyes as they seemed to rove past her, into the hall, over the oriental runner, to the cheese plant on the stand next to the painting of her grandmother's favourite poppies. The thought that he might push past her on his way to eat the tropical leaves momentarily frightened her. Then she remembered her grandfather's walking stick was on the coat stand. The last time he had used it was in a similar situation, being alone and helpless one stormy night when two travellers had called. Under the pretence of being lost and having wandered about in the snow, they attempted to gain admittance. The housekeeper of the time had spent hours scrubbing the blood off the floor the morning after. Yes, it strengthened her resolve to take action. They would receive nothing from this household.

Annie Tuckett took off her cap and gave it to her brother. She tried to say that he needed it because he had a cold, but Elizabeth slammed the door shut.

How dare they stand on the threshold with their diseases? She shouldn't be the one forced to answer the door. She'd only done so because she thought it might be the late delivery of a present from her favourite step-mother. And where was she? She obviously didn't care.

Where was everyone? She'd not had her Perrier water and it was gone seven o'clock. The whole situation was becoming unbearable.

She ran to the study, but no matter how hard she knocked, her father would not answer. The only other person in the house was the old butler. He was unarousable in his bed. Not dead, but full of laudanum.

In the attic room next door, she heard the ghostly mews of kittens.

It took some time for her to recover. Much later, in her room, surrounded by the objects that gave her comfort, did her reason return. She lay on her bed, clutching her red shoes, thinking of events long gone, and what yet could be. The house was still and the night was cold as she thought, and planned…

In the gloom of the small hours, in her nightdress and rag curlers, Elizabeth crept down the stairs to the kitchen, with her left-over sweetmeats. She lit a candle and stood on a chair, reaching to the top of the cupboard, and drew out the tin of strychnine. She knew where it was. For ten years it remained in the same place, exactly where she had put it back after using it the first time.

She silently mixed the powder into the treat she had prepared. Tonight, she would be rid of the reminder of her first misdemeanour. As a five-year-old, she'd not known the correct dose to finish off her rival. The lovely Isobel had liked to drink tea made from herbs picked in the field. It was easy, even for a child, to mix the substance in the pot, but what a pity her baby was delivered breathing. He should have died with her.

She carefully opened the door and went over to the little boy's bed.

It was empty, but for the dent where his bones had recently lain. At first, Elizabeth wondered if he was finally no more, and had been carried out by the ethereal step-mother and kittens that frequented her room in the dark.

She heard a scratching noise above her head. He was in the attic. Of course! It hadn't been restless ghosts, walking the floorboards, it had been him. He was more robust than she imagined.

It would be soon over. She'd mixed in enough poison this time to disintegrate his innards. Elizabeth smiled as she walked up the narrow creaking steps to the attic and quietly opened the junk room door. She thought she heard the scrabbling of tiny claws on floorboards, but the room was still. And there in the dark sat the little boy, in his chair, his head in his chest, looking up at her with his dark gypsy eyes. She walked over to him, holding out the plate, and said: 'Happy Christmas, dear brother..'

Mrs Miskin returned in the morning, walking in the snow that had fallen in the night. The house was cold and silent.

Mr Cummings slumbered in his chair in the study, and the children were nowhere to be seen. Elizabeth was not in her bed. The little boy was not in his room, the attic or the stable. Mrs Miskin called out the stable boy, Mr Rice (junior) and the young maid, all of whom were reluctant to trudge in the cold snow looking for lost children.

They were not to be found.

Mrs Miskin roused her master, who staggered around the house, found his bed and fell upon it.

It was a hopeless situation.

When the villagers were all eating their meagre dinners in their cold homes, the housekeeper scoured the snow-covered stables and the hedges.

It was a desperate situation.

There was blood on the floor in the attic, and tiny paw prints danced in the dust near a plate of sweetmeat.

In the churchyard, there was a half-covered set of single small footprints that led to Isobel Cummings's grave, then went back through the graveyard to the lane and out of the village, then disappeared.

When Mrs Miskin found a sharp knife in the stable, with blood on the blade, she called in the Constabulary.

Someone had left parcels outside the houses of the poorest in the village, very early on Christmas morning. Annie Tuckett had a pair of slightly worn red shoes and some beautiful silk ribbons, her brother had his hat returned.

For May Johnson there was a beautiful dress with a pink sash. Her father sold it and the family bought chickens which served them well for the next year with eggs and meat.

The Robinson family, whose shelves were bare and their

baby starving, had a fresh pig's heart that they feasted on at lunchtime. And old Mrs Spencer, the widow too infirm to work the fields, received two fresh kidneys which went in the pot on her fire.

It was quite a surprise. No-one expected such generosity, and everyone wondered whose feet left their mark in the snow. Saint Nicholas's were a lot larger.

No-one knew of the young boy who had raised his eyes up to the heavens the evening before and prayed for peace. Or of what happened after he went into the stable to feed the second litter of kittens the cat had given birth to, and found the sharp knife used to cut the hay twine (and the maid's corset ribbon), under the kittens' bed of straw.

Interlude

I hope you enjoyed the first part of this little book. Perhaps you see it as a pamphlet – a short treatise of a life – rather than a drawn out drama. That's how I'd describe my current situation. Let me explain.

I was hanging out my washing this morning, and Jeff opened his back door. Out came the dog, full pelt. Big Alsatian called Oy, I believe. It ran at the fence and cleared it. My life flashed in front of my eyes – what little I've done in it – but the brute went straight into my house.

My screams alerted Fred, the coalman who was just getting into his truck down the ten-foot. So he and Jeff go running around my house, leaving dirty bootmarks all over the living room, while I was outside, a gibbering jelly. They dragged the dog out. Jeff reluctantly apologised. I could see it in his eyes. The embarrassment. But that wasn't the end of it. Oy went into their house and barked non-stop in the living room, with just the wall between me and it, as I was trying to calm myself down with a brew and a ginger biscuit.

Then the scraping started.

How many layers of wallpaper are they taking off?

Annette came around – first time – and offered to help me clean up, but I told her what I thought. She gave me a very dark look, like *you'd better watch it*. I don't understand why people can't be civilised and give me some consideration. I just want a quiet life.

Now they have started banging on their side.

I think they're doing it to drive me out. Maybe they think I'm renting, like them. But George had a good job at the steelworks. He was in management, and we saved up enough to pay off the mortgage, before he went on that walk. He shouldn't have gone. He'd still be here if he hadn't.

I shouldn't get maudlin. My mother used to say there was no use moping around. If something's bothering you, do something about it. That's how I got into my geraniums. I bring them into the house in the autumn, and they flower right into winter. George used to say I was his little pelargonium.

Well, no-one is making me move out of my house. My friend Beatrice says I should go on a holiday. She means well. She's even said she'll go with me. Majorca, that's *the* place to go. On a jet plane. My dad was an engineer in the war. He said they're tin cans, put together with spit and duct tape. *If* I was going away, it'd be to Scarborough. There's plenty of sunshine there, and I wouldn't die in a terrible plane crash. But I'm not going. Why should they force me from my home? I'm staying put.

I am becoming concerned. I have told Marlene across the road. Her husband is a police officer. I also told Mrs Joplin at the newsagents. She expressed some sympathy, in between selling gobstoppers to the school children. She said I should speak to the police. I told her I'd already told Marlene. It's bad enough having the coalman and the dustman in. I don't want more boots on my cream shag pile.

Again, I digress. It's late, and they're still scratching away, but I won't let them get the better of me.

'Care about what other people think and you will always be their prisoner.'

That's a quote from Lao Tzu. He seemed to understand human nature.

I hope you enjoy the second story. I am just going to get my rolling pin…

Daemons

'Selfish creatures,
born from the basest
of human emotions.
Avoid at all costs. If
necessary, relocate
across a fast-flowing
river.'

Miss Johnson

It was a bleak Christmas Day morning. With the sun yet to rise, a cold wind swept across the fields bringing with it a storm of white flakes that covered the little boy and turned his cheeks to ice.

Around him was a raggedy coat that bulged in places. Often one of these lumps would move as kittens climbed in and out of hidden pockets, snagging his frozen skin.

The little boy walked through the snow all night, away from the village that did not know he even existed. In such weather, living things shuttered up their windows and blocked the drafts from doors, or curled themselves up into little balls under the hedges for shelter. It was folly to walk out, unless one was in a mind to pass on to the other side. But the little boy was beyond the living. He walked with a spirit, not knowing where it took him. Over gates, across frozen rivers, and past dark shapes of dwellings. The light that moved in front of him did not stop. And the boy faithfully followed.

He was tired now, hardly able to lift his feet. Barely able to keep his eyes open, he stumbled on in a flurry of flying snow. He did not see the dark shape of the little cottage ahead that marked the boundary of the village, and of a dark forest that lay across the bottom of the valley.

He finally halted at the woodshed that stood at the side of the dwelling. The light stopped, for a moment hovering in front of him, lighting up his face. Then it rose into the dark sky.

The exhausted little boy raised his hand in desolation, before tottering into the shed's doorway and collapsing onto a pile of hazel wood sticks, scattering the kittens amongst the logs and dust.

The cottage's resident was sound asleep when her young visitor arrived.

Miss Johnson was a seamstress, the only one in the village, and the only daughter of the deceased Edwin Johnson. He had been the Banker in the nearby town, which would not have pleased his distant ancestor: John, son of John of Etton who fell foul of the local moneylender when his crops failed and he could not repay his loan. There was an unfortunate incident after John's family were turned out of their cottage. A dark mean hut made of straw and dung. The money lender walked away with a bloodied nose. While the family were taken in by John's wife's sister Emma, daughter of Stephen of Beverley, John son of John drowned his sorrows with Emma's ale, sitting on a fallen log at the crossroad which was where the moneylender's men found him and swiftly removed the hand that struck their master.

This caused much upset amongst the villagers as John son of John was known as a decent man who did not work or sup ale on the Sabbath, and the moneylender felt it prudent to leave the area. He moved to Wallton. A grand town with many opportunities to lend gold.

Shortly after he settled in a solid timber house in the town, it was discovered that he was a moneylender, and they were not trusted by many people, particularly as a well-liked shoe-maker, with a large family had recently had his hand removed for striking the man who had demanded his loan repaid in full, with double interest. Unfortunately, the moneylender from Etton was mistaken to be the hand-remover and was quickly dispatched in front of an angry baying mob, by flame, and his possessions confiscated by the Town's officials. And unfortunately for the inhabitants of the steep Main Street, an uncontrollable fire from the incident spread quickly, destroying twenty-two houses, killing three people and one chicken in its wake.

Of these terrible events, Edwin Johnson was unaware when he chose his illustrious career, initially increasing the bank's revenue to the extent that his name shone as bright as the gold in its vaults. Unfortunately, his success was short-lived after encouraging the bank's investment in a cotton mill that caught fire and burnt to the ground, three ships that sank, and a soap mill that flooded. All the loans were unsecured.

With a reputation in tatters and a wife that loved shining necklaces, the hounds of liability were soon at the door, and the family found themselves accommodated at Beverley Debtors' Prison.

And this is where Edwin Johnson and his wife perished after a cholera outbreak, which diminished the prison population by half, most fortunate for the Governor of the establishment, who had previously underestimated the amount of gruel each inmate consumed whilst languishing around contemplating their fate.

Fortunately, young Miss Johnson, having caught a chill, was given ale as a restorative tonic by the Prison Chaplain's sister. The young girl had not drunk from the prison's water supply, the nearby river, into which many unnameable articles were disposed. The Prison Chaplain's sister also endowed her with some dressmaking skills before sending her out at thirteen, to take on the position of scullery maid at a big house in the Wolds. Cleaning hearths and scrubbing floors. A far cry from sweetmeats and oranges enjoyed by the girl two years previously.

The Cook discovered Miss Johnson's talent with a needle. The woman was in the habit of clearing the left-over fine food from the family table. After all, it was delicious, having been prepared by her own hand. Many a button was found in the gravy boat, and the custard tart, until young Miss Johnson let out her dress.

Servants with skills were much valued whilst their fingers and backs remained straight, and Miss Johnson was more prudent than her father. After a few years, she had the means to rent the little cottage at the edge of the village of Westhoplin, and left the big house in search of freedom and fresh air…

Miss Johnson woke on Christmas day, blue toes sticking through her well-darned stockings and a thick layer of ice on the inside of her window. She pulled on her worn shoes and went out to get wood, to stoke up the embers of the night's previous fire.

As she reached into the ramshackle lean to her hand grasped hold of something soft and warm. She could scarcely believe what she spied in the gloom. What luck! She scooped the little cat in her arms.

She pulled the bolt across the door of her home, holding the furry body tight against her ribs. No-one was taking this little one away from her. This creature was hers now. She had a fleeting idea of putting the kitten in the pot over the fire to add meat to her potatoes and carrots; but quickly dismissed it.

No, the cat was a gift to rid her of the vermin that was sharing her home.

She stoked up the fire, put on her shawl and bonnet, and went out in the snow to church to quench the fire of guilt. In her flurry of activity, she failed to see the pale face at the window.

The boy, too tired to lift a hand to the windowpane, slipped slowly down the wall outside and a slide of snow from the roof covered him from view as Miss Johnson left the cottage. He fell into a dark sleep.

Fortunately for him, the rest of the kittens were in his coat, and the warmth of their furry bodies kept his flickering light burning. The winter sun shone down on the snow that surrounded him.

Miss Johnson was rather disappointed with the day's sermon.

The Reverend Smedwick delivered a tempered message of Good Will to all Mankind and the Importance of Charity. He rejoiced at the Birth of Our Good Lord and raised some eyebrows with his beaming smiles at the congregation, from his raised pulpit, recently paid for by a raise in the parish tax. That wasn't the only thing villagers suspected their money was funding.

Whispers carried around the little church started by Mrs Spindle, the ironmonger's wife, sitting at the front with her razor sharp nose. She murmured to Mrs Tingle, the roofer's widow, that there was a presence of spirit about the Reverend, and it didn't smell like the holy type. When it reached Mrs Banks, the butcher's wife, in the third row she added that she had seen the Lady's maid from the Hall standing on the doorstep of the vicarage delivering a bottle in a paper packet into the Reverend's hands. Brandy she supposed, but it was too late to add to a seasonal fruit pudding.

The seamstress did not hear this. She sat next to old Mr Partridge who was as deaf as a snake, and therefore unable to partake in the weekly whispered conversations. She was disappointed with the subject of the lesson. Perhaps the Sunday sermon would contain his usual vigorous venom towards lost souls.

The sun seemed to be dimmer when Miss Johnson stepped out from the dark stone church, nodding solemnly, as was her way, at her fellow villagers, before setting off down the frozen track to her home.

She was looking forward to her potato and carrot soup, and the aroma of a delectable feast greeted her as she entered the cottage. The lid was off her cooking pot. She cursed herself for forgetting to put it on before she had left. Much of it had evaporated into the air, but there was enough to fill her bowl today.

Now where had it gone? She peered around her chair, the wonky wooden table on which she sewed, the pile of shirts and linen waiting to be mended. No bowl.

Then a movement on the bed caught her eye. At first she thought it was the cat, but it was weaving around her ankles, purring loudly. Her heart thudded in her chest, and the room shrank to a pinpoint as she focused on her rickety bed.

Something was IN it, moving about. Her blood chilled as a

guttural sound came from under the blanket.

The Reverend's Eve of Christmas sermon had focussed upon a man driven by base desires and eaten by avaricious demons that crawled down the walls and ripped him apart whilst he slept in his bed. Now one of these same creatures languished under her bed covers, with hot rancid breath and sharp talons.

It was waiting in there, to tear into her flesh and eat her heart.

Looking around for a weapon to defend herself with she picked up her broom. Brandishing it above her head she brought it swiftly down on the writhing figure. The empty jug, by the side of the bed, that had held her ale, went flying.

The cover drew back with a piercing shriek, matched by her own.

A small dark demon jumped out.

The noise was loud enough to disturb the pigeons sitting on the bare branches of nearby trees. They flew up in a flurry of grey, sprinkling Reverend Smedwick's head with the end product of frozen berries eaten earlier that morning.

He wouldn't have been under that particular tree at that moment if he hadn't stopped to rest his aching leg. His age, it would seem, was getting the better of him. And now it had started to rain.

The Reverend was on his way to the Wentworth farm, next to Miss Johnson's cottage, to deliver a bird kindly donated the day before by the Lady Whitlow from the Hall, following the loss of Mr Wentworth. The maid, a shy young girl, had hovered on the doorstep before thrusting the brown bag into his hand with the note from Lady Whitlow and scurrying away. It was a sad business, losing one's husband, with eight young children to feed, and an ailing bed-ridden mother who could only communicate by banging a stick against the floor. They had not yet found his body, nor that of the Smith's girl Isobel, who had disappeared the same night after going out to put the chickens away. It was rumoured that the last wolf in the country had carried her off in its jaws along with two chickens. Mr Smith had been most distressed about the loss of his poultry.

His other parishioners had been more concerned about the reported beast than any missing persons. It was said that its back was as long as young Mr Partridge's beer cart, fur as dark as the bottom of Westhoplin Gorge, and glowing yellow eyes as bright as the lamp the gravediggers carried. Such a description was enough to strike terror into any man walking alone at night on his way back from Legless Barghest public house, and indeed, bring about sobriety in the most hardened drinker, so Reverend Smethwick was averse to challenge it. But with the awful screaming he had heard from the seamstress's ramshackle cottage, he wondered if such a beast could exist.

He dropped the bag with the bird outside the door before he pushed it open, to avoid any confusion about gifts.

His fears of murder and mayhem diminished when he spied the back of Miss Johnson leant over the table with a carving knife. She was obviously about to cut up her dinner. A little ginger and white cat jumped around at her feet.

Hearing the door opening she turned, saw the Reverend and let out another ghastly scream. For a moment she looked like the demented gargoyle that stared down at him, when he stood in the pulpit, from the rafter above the third pew. The seamstress dropped the knife.

'Miss Johnson.' He stepped over the threshold. 'I am so sorry to frighten you. I heard a noise. It must have been an animal in the forest.'

He was disturbed by a sudden movement under the table. His eyes, adjusting to the gloom of the cottage, spied a pale face looking up at him. It was a dishevelled little boy, hunched up next to an empty bowl. His large dark eyes caught the Reverend in quiet sadness.

Reverend Smedwick was astonished. Miss Johnson, the isolated seamstress who communicated mainly through frosty stares and slight nods at Easter and Christmastide; who avariciously drank upon the fire and brimstone of his sermons from her seat on the fifth row, had taken in an orphan?

The woman looked bewildered. Her benevolent secret discovered. She was not the mean dried up stick that Mrs Spindle called her. Nor the miserable fiend that had thrown the Smith boy's wooden top into the river, because the noise of his happiness had irritated her senses. Or the one rumoured to have sewn the bottom of Maria Millicent's dress up when she heard the young woman had allegedly elicited favours from the newly married David Flint, including him helping her to strip the raspberry bush outside Miss Johnson's door. No, she was the personification of Charity.

Suddenly the floor was alive with rolling kittens, extracting themselves from the boy's clothing. Miss Johnson stood frozen to the spot, staring at the purple-haired Reverend who, regaining his composure, held out his hand to the little boy.

'Hello, little one.' To Miss Johnson: 'Pray what is his name?'

The boy turned his face to look at the seamstress. The Reverend's heart thudded heavily for a moment as he looked into the wide dark eyes. Beneath the boy's tattered cloak was a velveteen dress coat with silver buttons and a greyed lace collar. Here was a poor soul fallen upon hard times, with his life yet begun.

Miss Johnson was also enrapt. She wondered how the small demon she had been chasing up the walls and under the table could so swiftly transform itself. Could it be she was in presence of a younger version of the fiend Deacon Brodie, now showing a face of respectability under the gaze of an emissary from God? Then again, she remembered seeing a picture of the Archangel Gabriel - crude and dark in its depiction, painted by an artist in the prison. Mr Bramble. He said he had painted the Mayor of Beverley, and Lord Etton before he was taken up with derby days.

'Sometimes angels come to us in dark clothing,' he had told her young self.

Mr Bramble had been arrested by five of the constabulary on a particularly windy day as he fled his debtors. They had come at him, cloaks billowing out like dark wings that he had thought they were demons. He was so frightened he'd not seen the open trap door of the cellar to the Crooked Shilling Public House and broke both his legs in the fall. 'But I never put another farthing on anything after that,' he'd said. 'Those dark messengers saved me from Hell. Now I sit in Arcadia.' Once his legs had healed, he was able to climb up to the window and look out on the landscape of Beverley Westwood, and would sketch cows on the walls, until the Chaplain got him engrossed in biblical depictions for the prison church.

But the Reverend Smedwick waited expectantly for a name, whilst Miss Johnson was caught up in irrelevant past memories. She pondered on this. Would an angel-demon possess such a thing?

'Edward'' she said. 'His name is Edward.'

The silence was broken by a clear young voice. 'My name is Alfred.'

'Edward Alfred.' Miss Johnson finished.

'God Bless you both!' Reverend Smedwick removed a small bag from his belt. 'Please accept this gift Miss Johnson. I believe we have some clothes at the Vicarage that might be more appropriate for this time of year. And we can waive the fee for schooling, just bring him the day after tomorrow. We do not provide lunch, but we do have chalk and a slate.'

Miss Johnson composed herself and took the bag from him, nodding.

'I will bring him, Sir Reverend.'

Outside the door the Reverend picked up the bag he had dropped and threw it over his shoulder. It felt strangely warm against his back, and seemed to move, but he dismissed this as his imagination which seemed quite stimulated this Christmas Day. As he walked, he formulated an idea for his Boxing Day service: Angels walking amongst men. No eternal damnation, that could wait until the New

Year. And he would focus upon the evil of drink, and fix his stare upon Mr Spindle, sitting at the front of the church on Christmas Day, smelling like a distillery.

The Wentworth family was delighted with the kitten that jumped out of the bag that the Reverend placed on the table. It was a strange gift from Lady Whitlow but would kill the rats that ran around the children's feet.

The goose had rolled out of the bag into the snow drift by the window, and the cheeky cat, smelling raw meat had clambered inside to lick the delicious tasting sacking. His little life was perfect, in a warm room, surrounded by lots of smiling faces and little hands that cuddled and stroked him. He would get fat eating the rodents he killed.

In the cottage the atmosphere was somewhat different.

Miss Johnson broke from her frozen pose and picked up the knife she had been brandishing. The little boy tasted fear yet again. The woman was strange, with her shrieking, wild eyes and her bent back. He could think of no reason to stay and deeply regretted eating her meal.

He wanted to apologise, but she was looking at the bag the Reverend had left and tipped it out onto the table. Four potatoes and three carrots rolled out.

Miss Johnson looked quite mad as she laughed, knife in hand, holding up a potato in the air. The little boy scrambled to his feet and took to the door. On the way out, he tripped and fell, hitting his head on the goose.

When he opened his eyes, he saw the glint of a sharp blade. The strange thin woman's green eyes were close to his. His heart pounded so hard that he saw little white stars all around the wild woman's face.

He winced as a hand came down to his head. He knew he would hurt…

But Miss Johnson picked up the goose laid beside the boy. Was this what he had carried here wherever he came from? Was he indeed, and angel in disguise? Now she faced a conundrum.

She had lived so many years in solitude and she liked it. There had been no-one to talk to or who made unnecessary noise; no one that would require character training and bring constant disappointment. If he had been a girl, it might have been different. She could tolerate a prim little child in a dress. She could have taught her how to make lace. Instead, there would be a fidgeting, smelly, potentially rude boy, like the ones that threw stones at her window and ducked away from her broom. She was quite uncomfortable with the weight of words that tumbled through her head.

If the Reverend hadn't burst in when he did, she could be peeling her potatoes in peace, with the urchin sent on his way. And now there was a promise to a man of the cloth.

'You will have to sleep on the floor near the fire,' she said, defeated. 'Best go in and peel the potatoes. How did this bird come to be here?'

The boy picked himself up and brushed away the snow from around his mouth. He had dark eyes, like the tramp that used to come to her employers' back door, asking for scraps of food all those years ago. She'd caught that one trying to steal the copper kettle off the stove. There was always an issue with strangers.

She would keep the knife under her pillow, and her ale hidden in the log shed.

Reverend Smedwick walked back to the Vicarage pondering on his day. It was strange that a goose should turn into a cat, but it was much welcomed by the Wentworth's. Curious too that there were chicken bones in the cesspit when they had no animals, and the children looked rosy-cheeked and healthy after a week without food.

It was also peculiar that Miss Johnson should take in a little waif. He had seen another side to her today, this most special day. With a little guidance, she would make a generous and kind mother, of that he was sure.

Another Interruption

The police have been to see me.

I thought at first it was Marlene, or maybe Mrs Joplin. No, it was 'Mr and Mrs Brown.'

'Mr and Mrs Brown?' I said. 'Who are they?'

Jeff and Annette.

They reported *me* for making nuisance noises.

I was so upset PC Bramham had to give me his handkerchief. I showed them the polystyrene tiles I've had to put on the walls, and explained about all the stress I've been through, since my husband died on a walk in the Dales. That brought it all back. He fell in a river he was trying to cross. They found the bag with his sandwiches and flask of tea, washed up further down-stream. Apparently, it was a popular place to try to jump across, and some people don't make it. They should cordon it off. Blow it to smithereens with dynamite.

PC Bramham was very sympathetic. He said they would look into my complaint as well. I asked if they could phone me, rather than just turn up on the doorstep. That way I can brew the tea properly in the pot. PC Bramham likes his tea strong.

I had to tell them about the dog as well. I hope that Oy is well looked after. I don't blame him – apart from the piddle he did against the living room wall he seemed quite harmless in the end.

I did such a lot of talking, I really feel I embarrassed myself. But I've not opened up like that since Jean lived next door. She was a wonderful listener, never judgemental. You wouldn't expect that from an older lady, but she was rather special. I was very sad when she went.

I think I overstepped the line when I told PC Bramham that. I mean, it's got nothing to do with 'Mr and Mrs Brown's' affairs. He probably found it irrelevant. But he does have the most remarkable brown eyes.

He will be back, I'm sure. I have his handkerchief, and perhaps a little more…

Although I don't know if a young woman in my situation needs the attention of a man such as he. I can't see anything good coming out of it.

I've proven I am capable (even though George disagreed). I've got myself a job, I pay the bills, keep the house clean, and have even taken up some more manual work. My skills in bricklaying are quite adequate. The wall is still intact, and it's taken quite a beating – from my rolling pin.

It is regrettable that Jean had to go. She was so much better than my mother, for listening I mean, although towards the end she was becoming quite interested in my DIY.

I've kept her near to me, in my heart.

I have every faith in PC Bramham. I am sure he will sort out this situation, all the drama will stop, and I'll be able to look at my mother's stories again.

I'm afraid I will have to distance myself now, from people. The ones I asked for help from didn't do anything. The scratching is lessening now. I didn't tell PC Bramham that, I was too upset about all the accusing that was going on.

I expect they'll be finished soon, and it will be quiet again. I'll be relieved. I've quite had enough of them – the people behind the wall.

Wierged Wulf

'Accursed wolf. A bite from
such a beast brings the
infection. It goes without saying,
you should not approach
unknown hairy dogs or humans.
And you cannot outrun them.'

The Last Wolf

I t was a cold, cruel winter in the Wolds village of Westhoplin.

The seamstress' cottage was full of bodies, jostling to be near the fire. The little boy, the thin seamstress (whose face was becoming more pinched as she considered her changed circumstances), and four furry bodies jumping and bumping around, sticking their little pin claws into the lady's stockings.

As she settled down for the night, Miss Johnson could scarcely believe that morning she had risen merely with the thought of feeding herself through the winter. And by the evening she had, through the Reverend Smedwick's goodwill, adopted a stray child, four kittens, and a dead goose.

The little boy slept on a small rug by the fire with the kittens curled around him. They slumbered deeply, leaving the dark memories of the Cummings's stable behind them, dreaming in the warmth with full bellies.

The next morning, Miss Johnson rose to a fresh fall of snow and icicles that ran frosted fronds across the inside of the window. Today was the second day of Christmastide. Somewhere, in the thread of time, she remembered her father on this day would give gratuities to the servants. They were things from the house, unwanted items. The chipped pot, the leaking bucket, the cloak with no pin, boots with holes on the soles.

They were grateful, these poor attendants. They had nothing, and would gain nothing from these gifts, but she remembered how they thanked him and wished him the luck he deserved.

There were no gratuities for her here. The villagers whose socks she darned, and buttons she sewed back on, had nothing.

That day, she stoked up the fire, and they ate the rest of the goose with the potatoes.

The boy stayed in the corner where he was told. The kittens tripped her up at every step. She was quite tempted at one point to throw them on the fire, but the boy's dark eyes seemed to burn into her skin, like the demon that had taken the erring sinner.

He didn't speak much, the little raggedy stranger.

'I don't know,' seemed to be the stock answer.

She wondered what creature she had welcomed into her home. He seemed to shrink like a shadow in the midday sun when she gazed upon him, and he had dark stains on his collar, like he'd eaten some very ripe berries. There were some that grew in the woods. Pokeberries. Good for expelling everything. She hoped he hadn't. It would make a mess on the floor when the purging started. Then she hoped he had. Enough consumed and there wouldn't be another mouth to feed, clothes to find, a blanket to share.

One day had barely passed, and she already felt the rumble of discontent with the Reverend and his potatoes.

It was another cold night, and when she awoke the strains of a weak rising sun were filtering through the tiny window.

The boy did not lie in a pool of vomit. She was somewhat disappointed, and more so when she surveyed the interior of her home.

The pan on the fire was empty, and the woodshed was bare. She had been overzealous in her kindness; but Christmas was now over.

The cats would have to go. There was nothing for them to eat. She contemplated her resolution. She couldn't drown them in the river in a sack. She had used her last one to cover the sprouts she was trying to grow. Perhaps Mr Pike the handyman from the Hall could hit them with his spade? She'd have to go out while the deed was committed, and the boy would have to be engaged in a task, such as gathering sticks. It seemed quite desperate, but she could make gloves from the fur.

She mused over her plan for a while and became rather pained in her stomach. It was probably the goose. Maybe she should just shut them outside. They could fend for themselves.

She jumped as one of them stretched suddenly, swiping the boy's nose, waking him up. Now the busy day had begun.

It was the little boy's first day at school. Miss Johnson started the arduous task of cleaning him up. Although she knew his name, she thought he looked more like an 'Archibald', with his dark curly hair and pale frost-pinched face. A good, upstanding name. She pulled his collar straight and combed his hair.

Reverend Smedwick had asked Mr Smith a farm worker to send his son Tom to make sure the orphan found his way to the school. He'd barely knocked when Miss Johnson pushed the little boy out into the snow and shut the door.

Tom looked him up and down. He'd been expecting a more robustly attired fellow student and was anxious at the way his lumpy jacket moved. He'd sat next to a boy last year with pustules that had suddenly burst and covered him in stinking yellow slime. He'd been dunked immediately in a bath and covered in lime that burned him. It made him wary of new boys, but the Reverend had promised his father a coin on completion of the day, and they never had such a thing before, so he was bound to his task. If not completed, he would get a good beating from his dad.

Then he saw a little furry face appear from under the boy's jacket. His anxiety increased.

'What's that? A kitten! Are you taking it to school? You can't take it to school! Mr Dowson won't let you in with animals. Oh, there's another! Mr Dowson will give us both a caning.'

Tom thought the boy was going to cry, but he scooped up the kittens. It looked like he was going back to Miss Johnson's. Tom had to stop him.

'For me?' He stepped up to the little boy. 'I've always wanted two cats. They'll keep each other company. Let's take them to my mam.'

He snatched them off the little boy and ran all the way back to the little cottage where his family lived, at the other side of the wood. Their cat was found dead in the snow a few days ago, in a pool of blood. A fox, a large one by the look of it. Mrs Smith gave the little boy a hunk of bread. Mrs Spindle had told her that the frigid Miss Johnson would probably be keeping him in the shed, so she wouldn't have to share her potatoes.

The little boy was threatened and pushed along the path through the wood, to the centre of the Westhoplin, where stood the place of worship, next to the mansion of learning.

The school house looked like a cattle shed, with its low roof and damp wood cladding, except there were children instead of cows and chickens. Rows of silent young pupils at small wooden desks, and a tall man, dressed in a black suit with a disapproving stare.

Mr Dowson the school teacher had the pleasure of being a relation to Lady Witlow. His only one, having recently fallen upon harder times. 'Disappointing' was his most regularly used word. It related to most aspects of his life.

He surveyed the rabble of young paupers assembled in the dingy room and brought his wooden ruler sharply down on the desk in front of him, usually vacant for this very reason, but now occupied by a startled-looking gypsy urchin.

'First lesson of the day. The difference between Right and Wrong.'

Miss Johnson spent her morning out in the woods, looking for berries. An unsatisfying meal, but such was her seasonal diet. The snow was deep and there was a chill in the air. She followed tracks of little animals, hoping they had left something after their foraging. As she walked, she found some strange marks in the snow, paw prints, larger than a fox's. They crossed the array of human boot marks. She wondered if one of the farmers had gained a large hound over Christmastide. Probably Mr Tiller. He was light-fingered. Always stealing sheep, then saying it was the wolf. Or Mr Smith. He always had a shifty look about him.

She was disturbed in her musing by Mrs Spindle who was out looking for her husband. He'd not come home the night before. Initially, she had been pleased about this. A night free of snoring and slobbering in the bed. Mrs Spindle apologised to Miss Johnson for her not having the opportunity to be married, therefore not able to understand the finer aspects of wedlock. Mrs Spindle explained she had remained content that day, until Mr Pike the handyman from the Hall had arrived asking about Lady Witlow's bed knobs. Now she needed her carpenter husband and he was missing.

She told Miss Johnson about her great disturbance. Passing through a copse earlier she had discovered a load of raw meat dumped in a pool of blood. If people were to dispose of the remains of poaching, she would appreciate if it was done more discretely, such as in the Smith's ditch. She went on and on about ruffians and stolen chickens, leaving Miss Johnson's thoughts to wander. Perhaps Mr Spindle had found the pokeberries, and lay somewhere in a drift, completely purged? But he was a drunkard, and if anything, he'd be laid in a drift, full of the Legless Barghest's best brew.

With what remained of the season's goodwill, Miss Johnson wished her neighbour felicitations and continued her search for dinner. Tramping through the snow, she came across the copse with the remains. Unfortunately, most of it had been taken by wild animals, but as she turned to go, her boot caught on something buried in the snow. It was so near the shredded remains of entrails, she was initially averse to investigate, but glad when she did. It was a chicken, frozen solid, but intact. Had someone buried it here, to retrieve later? With no one around, she slipped it under her coat and furtively returned home.

By the time the little boy came back, the house smelled of the bird, cooking in its juices in the pot. When she asked where the other two kittens had gone, he scowled most unbecomingly, and said that Tommy Smith had relieved him of them.

He also said he wasn't going to school any more.

Harold Pouch from High farm, whilst looking for a lost sheep in the wood early the next morning, found a hand sticking out of a drift close to a copse with blood-stained snow. Unfortunately, it was not attached to a body. It was not known if it had previously belonged to Mr Wentworth, or Mr Spindle. It was too large to be that of Miss Smith's. He and Dr Tail took the item to the house of the most recently absent, and confirmed it to be that of Mr Spindle, before his wife slipped to the floor in an unconscious state.

How he was relieved of one of his most prized possessions (he always told Mrs Spindle he would be finished if he lost any of his appendages), and where the rest of him was located remained a mystery. Now almost all the villagers were out, looking for handless men, and missing girls.

All but Miss Johnson, who was escorting a reluctant boy to school, through the melting snow, recanting her missed opportunities of education at his age, being in the Debtor's Prison with her family. He was a lucky child, and he should not forget that.

'No-one will want a boy to mend their petticoats and drawers,' she said. 'Reading and writing pave the way to such worthwhile careers in banking or teaching.'

On the way back, and a way beyond, she discovered a shrub of bilberries in a remote spot. It overhung at the gorge where Lord Whitlow had met with his unfortunate accident four years previously. It was fortunate she was three miles away from her cottage, leaning over a cliff, as the search party traced a suspect pair of footsteps through the wood to her very doorstep.

Miss Johnson wrapped the berries in her handkerchief and

started back towards the village. As she walked through the woods, she became aware that she was not alone. Something moved within the trees, keeping pace with her hurried steps. Now, Mrs Tingle always said a woman should never go walking without a good sturdy cane. She was right. When anyone is being stalked by something in the trees, it's always good to have a stick at hand. In this case, a sharpened one.

She did find a fallen branch, somewhat wonky, but sturdy enough to smack someone across the head with.

'Who's there?' she asked, brandishing her weapon. 'Show yourself.'

'Miss Johnson,' came a quiet voice from behind a tree. 'I'm afraid I can't.'

'Mr Wentworth? Is that you?'

It was indeed. The artisan who had been missing for the last few days bobbed his head out from the undergrowth. Miss Johnson was immediately suspicious. This was not his usual manner. And where had he been all this time?

A quick march up to the tree revealed all. Despite the inclement weather, he was dressed only in his underwear, and that was, well, in need of a good bath.

And now he was most disconcerted.

'How dare you!' He attempted to cover himself with a dead fern. 'Get back behind that tree, woman!'

She gave him her shawl, which was very chivalrous, but he complained about the size of the crocheting and the draft it let through. As the cold wind bit, Miss Johnson regretted that the stick she had chosen was not sharpened. He continued to complain. About the wind, the snow, and the hunger. What did she have in her handkerchief that stained it so red?

Because they were on their own, and he was a big man, she placated him by poking her stick into his stomach and asking where he had been the past few days. He had been missed in church on Christmas day.

He stopped, near the edge of the gorge, leaning on a stump because his bones ached, and he felt a little sick; and told the thin seamstress his story.

As she knew, there were eight of them at home. Clem, Jem, and Ben. John, Jen, Ann and Sam.. and the one with the ginger hair. Anyway, he would not dispute the fatherhood of the eighth. That was another story.

He was out collecting wood for the fire… This she suspected as a lie, by the nervous look he gave her… Before he knew it, it was dark, and he was wandering across the Smith's field, when he heard a terrible howling. Something moved in the ditch, and when he got near, he saw it. The wolf, Miss Johnson, big grey thing, it was, foaming at the mouth, and looking at him with its light eyes. It was caught in one of those traps Smith littered about the place. He'd nearly stepped in one the week before, carelessly placed near the highway.

But back to the creature. It got angry upon seeing Mr Wentworth and showed its sharp teeth. He realised Isobel Smith stood behind it. That stupid little girl was trying to free it. How she'd not been eaten was beyond him. And she shouted at Mr Wentworth to stay away. She was rescuing the last wolf.

Her father, daft as he was, made his traps good, and all she did was give the creature more pain with the pulling and twisting she did. It turned on her and bit her arm. She ran off crying into the forest. With her out of the way he was able to despatch the creature. In a most humane manner. But the wolf sank its teeth into his leg with its dying gasp, and its eyes stared into his in such a strange way, he almost felt a twinge of guilt, but for the fact that he was a hero for slaying such a beast.

He looked down at the mark on his exposed thigh. A mere scratch, Miss Johnson thought.
He went off home with the chickens... 'I found them wandering in the field. They looked a bit mauled, that's why I took them. I fell asleep in my bed, and next thing I know, I was out here.'

'Why haven't you gone back home?' Miss Johnson was aghast. 'They're looking for you, and Miss Smith, and Mr Spindle.'

'I can't go back like this,' he said. 'The missus already thinks I've been doing more than tanning with my new assistant, Mary Moore. It's not true. She won't pure the leather, that girl. She says it's disgusting; she'll only wax. Do you, Miss Johnson, have anything I can wear?' His bright eyes roved over her dress, and in the fading light, she fancied she saw a bit of a beast in him.

'Mr Wentworth,' she said. 'You have had all the clothing I would part with. The rest you will have to wrestle from me, and I am loath to allow you that pleasure.'

He dipped his head. Behind him, a large yellow moon was rising in the sky. It shone like a crown about his dishevelled head, casting a yellow light across his eyes.

She now realised she had ventured too far from home. And it was too late. The little boy would be making his way home from school and she wasn't there stirring the chicken soup. Being rather more anxious than usual, she prodded the gentleman in his stomach, less gently this time.

He sprang back. Had his legs lengthened in the past few seconds?

'Miss Johnson,' he said. Now he was aghast. 'You mistake my intentions. I would never think of—really! With you? I'd rather..'

He seemed to go into a spasm. She not noticed before how hairy his face seemed. He'd let himself go, these past few days.

'I'd rather..'

And his hands, held up in front of him, displaying nails that he would need an axe to cut short. Miss Johnson watched, unable to move as the tanner twisted in freakishness.

'I'd rather..' His voice was becoming guttural. His eyes suddenly fixed hers. 'Eat your heart.'

She dropped the berries on the snow and staggered backwards. Mr Wentworth crouched down low, his hairy face leered at her in a most grotesque manner (like the rent collector who came every month and tried to offer her a discount 'for a favour'). Her stick lay on the ground by her foot, clumsily discarded in her panic.

She realised now… with the light almost gone, and her eyes not so good with all the mending she'd done… It wouldn't be her character that would suffer besmirchment at his hairy hands. He thought she had a pig's heart in her handkerchief and had a mind to steal it from her.

He really was a disgusting man. He lusted after young girls in the village. He'd not changed his underwear for a while. Who knows where he had performed his ablutions? He'd killed the last wolf, whilst it lay injured and trapped. And now he would steal her berries.

Her eyes went from the stick to the berries, her thoughts jumping about uncontrollably. Which one to pick up?

The berries. He wasn't taking them from her without a fight; she had walked miles to get them.

She went down quickly to pick up her handkerchief, and felt something whoosh past the top of her head, and then an agonising howl as Mr Wentworth landed right on the edge of the cliff. She'd not realised how adept a man with so many ulcers on his lower legs could be. As she looked at him, clutching her berries to her chest, he wobbled. For a moment, he froze, with an arm reaching out towards her. Then he lost his balance, and with a somewhat desperate look in his yellow eyes, fell three hundred feet down into the ravine landing on top of the bones of Lord Whitlow. It was common knowledge that the landowner had met his demise whilst out on a lone hunting trip, and that his body was irretrievable because of the narrow gorge sides. Anyone who had got down there would have found Lady Whitlow's plumed hat, having fallen off when she pushed him over the edge, after he had discovered she preferred gentlemen with bushy sideburns, such as the ones sported by Mr Pike, the handyman.

'Mr Wentworth,' Miss Johnson called down. 'Are you all right?' Her shock turned into anxiety when all she heard was the distant howl of a dog echoing through the forest. What was she to do now? It would be most awkward, having to explain to a Police Constable that the tanner had turned into a delinquent bone-grubber within the short time he'd lived almost naked in the forest in winter, before losing his footing trying to steal her berries. All for the sake of suspecting the latest child was not his. It wouldn't make any sense.

Meanwhile, the little boy was walking home from school, on his own, having been forsaken by Tommy Smith, who would receive no reward that evening for escorting him back safely.

The little boy had no furry companions to warm him and felt quite alone as he walked through the dark trees.

Today Mr Dowson had talked about Morals, Dignity and Restraint, and had hauled him in front of the class for drawing a dog on his slate board, instead of writing numbers. He couldn't identify any 'compassion' Mr Dowson had talked about as the man was spelling out 'disgusting' as he had brought his ruler down on the little boy's knuckles:

'D-i-s-g-u-s-t-'

'Hello?'

A young voice that came from the shadow of a nearby tree interrupted his thoughts.

A figure, no bigger than he stepped out onto the path. A girl. Her hair was loose and tangled, falling down over her shoulders. She wore a dirty petticoat. He looked away quickly, having been informed by Mr Dowson that little boys should not look at girls' underwear.

He felt a pressure on his arm. She stood next to him. Her light eyes glowed in the fading light.

'My name is Belle,' she said. 'What's yours?'

That was an interesting question. He now found himself to have three names.

'Boy,' he said. To save some trouble.

'Unusual,' she frowned. 'But can you help me? I'm lost in the woods. That is, I know where I live, but every time I try to get there, I fall asleep and wake up miles away.' She blushed a little, then continued. 'I live on the farm with the chickens, and my brothers Tommy and Ren.'

The little boy hesitated. Tommy Smith. He knew where he lived.

The girl took his hand. Hers was hot with energy, warming his cold skin like a fire.

She looked at him in a funny way.

'Are you a ghost?' she said.

'No.' He'd been called a lot of things, but not that.

She took his other hand too, and he winced because it hurt.

'What happened to you?' Her eyes glowed yellow as she stared at his damaged knuckles.

'I went to school.'

She nodded. Here, in her face was this 'compassion' Mr Dowson had spoken of. An unspoken understanding. Had she felt the surface of the ruler?

'Will you help me get home?' she asked.

He agreed. It was not far. He could stand at the fence and watch her go in, then return to the thin seamstress's cottage where his two furry companions would be waiting.

He thought it strange that she should fall asleep outside, as she said, particularly with a wind that niggled through to the bone.

'Do you know my brother?' She talked as they walked. 'Tommy. He goes to school too. But he doesn't come home with broken hands. I used to go, but Dad said girls shouldn't be educated. We should be at home, tending chickens. I don't like Mr Dowson, but I liked learning my grammar better than I like looking after chickens.' She seemed to quite enjoy talking, so he didn't interrupt.

'Three days ago,' she said. 'My mam sent me out after the chickens. They were running around the field. I saw a wolf. He was standing in the middle of the field. Dad says there haven't been wolves for centuries, but we've been seeing this one every now and again. He doesn't usually go for chickens. He likes to hunt. I think he likes to stretch his legs for his dinner.' She smiled brightly at the boy. Behind her, the moon rose winter yellow. 'I left him a chicken. There's not much to go after in the woods this time of year. He was very hungry. When he'd finished, we walked to the ditch. I was telling him where the traps were. He looked at me with his big yellow eyes like he knew what I was saying. Mr

Dowson says animals are dumb, but I don't think so. I don't think you think so either.'

He agreed, but he was becoming wary. Something didn't feel quite right. The wind had become still; the trees had stopped their whispers.

'Then Mr Wentworth, the tanner came running across the field with two birds in his hands. He got a right fright when he saw me with a big animal and turned tail. I think Mr Wolf saw his opportunity for a chase so off he went and caught him. It was a good tackle, but I thought people might be upset if Mr Wentworth got eaten by the last wolf, so I ran over and told Mr Wolf to go away. He was angry at being disturbed so close to his dinner that he nipped me, and Mr Wentworth ran off, not looking back to see how I was.' She scowled and showed her sharp white teeth. 'Mr Wolf decided that chicken tasted nicer than me. He made off with the best layer we have. I knew Dad would be mad about it, so I thought I'd walk for a bit. Wait 'till he'd gone to bed, and- what's wrong with you?'

The little boy had stopped, watching something moving in the trees. He didn't know what to think of wild animals, having spent most of life in the attic, but he knew what it felt like to be hungry. If that was the reason something was stalking them, he didn't want to be the main course.

She pulled his hand.

'Come on,' she said. 'I'm sure I will make it tonight, Boy. Walk with me a little longer. There'll be an end to it soon.'

He was sure there would be and hesitated. The shadow was moving toward them, rustling.

'Come on, Boy,' she said. 'We can run faster than them.' She pulled him along. 'You don't want to be bitten by a wolf, do you?'

He didn't, but neither did he want to go off the path with her. Wild as he was, she seemed strangely feral, with her hairy little shoulders, and sharp pointed nose. And now he realised that the feet that blustered over the dead twigs in the dark wood were too heavy to be lupus paws.

Mr Smith burst onto the path ahead of them, red-faced and

breathless. He brandished a pitchfork and shouted:

'Get away from my daughter, you scoundrel.'

The boy gladly stepped away. She had been looking at him and licking her lips with a long pink tongue. Now she looked at her father.

'Dad,' she said. 'We were only playing.'

'Where have you been for three days, and where are your clothes, girl? Get away with you!' He gesticulated at the boy who took flight, running through the trees. At a safe distance he paused and looked behind him. Two figures stood framed by trees, caught in an embrace. Then the larger one fell back onto the forest floor. The little boy stopped a scream and ran as fast as he could back to the seamstress's cottage, tripping, slipping, sliding through the icy snow.

Miss Johnson arrived home to a large crowd gathered outside her woodshed. The mood was ugly. The first thing they did was call her a witch. She wasn't sure who shouted it out. Mrs Tingle, or Mrs Spindle? Or why they would call her something she wasn't.

'Where's my husband?' Mrs Spindle said.

'And my daughter,' from Mrs Smith.

'I don't know,' Miss Johnson said. 'But I know where Mr Wentworth is.'

They didn't listen to her. Suddenly there were faces almost pushed against hers, accusing her of being a murderer.

Into the midst of this rabble ran the little boy, over to Miss Johnson, breathless and crying.

'Mr Smith. Belle. Bleeding on the ground. In the wood.'

Some in the crowd took this to be a confession and surged forward.

'This all started when he arrived.' 'It's him. And her. Can you smell what's cooking?' 'They're eating Mr Wentworth.'

Miss Johnson caught hold of the little boy. It looked like things could turn violent.

'We've done nothing,' she said.

'What *are* you cooking?' asked Mr Dowson.

'Chicken.'

'Chicken?' The stern man squared up to her. 'When did you acquire a bird?'

'We've had two, Sir,' the little boy said politely. He was keen to demonstrate his grasp of Truthfulness.

'Weren't there two chickens taken from the Smiths?' 'And their daughter.' 'Yes, Isobel too.'

Mrs Smith stepped forward. 'Where's my daughter?'

'She's with her father,' said the little boy.

'They've got him too.'

'Murderers!'

They grabbed the little boy and Miss Johnson. There was a lot of confusion. Flaming torches were being waved around. People were shouting.

Then a dark hairy figure wearing a dirty petticoat leaped out from behind a tree and jumped on Mr Dowson. Mrs Smith standing nearby was suddenly covered in blood, and Mrs Tingle discovered a severed head lying next to her foot.

Lots of people were screaming, and Miss Johnson found herself free. She grabbed the little boy and pushed him into the house, bolting the door.

The crowd gathered itself under the direction of Mr Browning, the Postmaster, and took off in the direction the strange beast had gone, leaving the seamstress's cottage.

They spent the night huddled together near the fire, with the two kittens; Miss Johnson held them all tight until the sun rose.

She had never liked the village of Westhoplin, nor its inhabitants the full ten years she had lived there, so she packed up a few items, wrapped the little boy and the kittens in her blanket, and they set off on the track that led out from the village, towards... anywhere but there.

Reverend Smedwick awoke the next morning, under the hedge on Lady Whitlow's lawn, bereft of his clothing. Isobel Smith was next to him, in her petticoat, her hand gently stroking his hair, as one would a pet dog.

'Hush Mr Wolf,' she said. 'We can go home. We're safe.

For another month.'

Finishing Lines

I'm done with crying.

PC Bramham has gone.

He left me with WPC Crouch. Her capabilities are doubtful. I mean, how can you protect people against criminals with a skirt that short?

I still can't believe what has happened. Those two next door—such horrible people. They've cast aspersions over my character.

It started this morning. I was emptying my twin tub when he came calling. PC Bramham, I mean. I told him I had just washed his handkerchief, and it would soon dry, with it being a nice day. He had such a stern face on. At first I thought he was here to tell me that Uncle Kenneth was dead. He's been in and out of hospital for a while with his head. He will tell everyone that he's the Queen Mother's cousin and has been to the future where people walk around with telephones in their pockets. How peculiar is that? I'd be tripping over all the wires when I went out shopping.

Anyway, PC Bramham said he needed to talk to me, and I thought I saw something in his eyes. I wondered if he'd been thinking of me last night while he tried to sleep. I would have put the kettle on, but he said he didn't want one, and there was an important reason for his visit. I thought I saw passion in those warm dark eyes and got quite flustered when it turned out he was here in his professional capacity. I think his button has gone under the cupboard.

Whilst he was straightening himself up, he delivered his blow. The Browns had called him again. I don't know why they are so unreasonable. All I want is to be left alone. Not that I could hear what he was saying all that well, with Oy barking through the wall. And he told me to stay against the cooker where he'd put me after the… misunderstanding. I pointed out the distracting noise, and he said, loudly, that he had an Alsatian too. I'd imagined he would have a deeper pitch when aroused, but he sounded like the siren that rings at the steelworks' home time. It wails right across the town. When I hear it, I always remember my mother putting on her coat and telling my brother to wrap me up and go to the shelter in the garden.

He was backing into the living room, whilst I was explaining Jeff and Annette's motives for getting rid of me.

It has become obvious that they dislike an attractive woman of independent means living next door. It's a threat.

PC Bramham said there might be some truth in what I was saying, although he did not believe the shape of anyone's eyebrows determined their character or demeanour.

When he got to the other side of the settee, he commented on how much smaller this room was, compared to next door.

I asked if Annette had made him a cup of tea, whilst they misrepresented the facts, sitting in their front room.

I believe at this point he was about to leave. His hand was on the front door. But his eyes were on my wall tiles, and his brain was, I fear, deducing, interpreting and misconstruing.

I suppose if I hadn't lost my rag, it might be different, but I said my husband had erected the wall. He liked to sit in a square room. We all have our foibles, don't we? He took out the curved bay. He preferred straight lines, did George.

PC Bramham was silent, but in his eyes an energy was awakening. I decided to feed it.

I wondered aloud if the noise that bothered both sides of the wall, could originate under the floorboards, on their side.

'It would be amusing, would it not, PC Bramham, if it turned out to be a colony of rodents?'

He said that 'the Browns' had taken up floorboards and found nothing underneath. I could see his eyes were bright with ideas. Then he asked about the last time I'd seen Jean.

I thought he was jumping ahead of himself. Jeff and Annette moved in a long time after Jean had left. But I went along with it. I might regain some of my humour if the police started pulling up the floorboards next door.

I just wanted to be left alone.

He became animated and really rather forceful. I like strong men. There are too many skinny ones with their long hair, high heels, and makeup. I don't know what the world's coming to with this Glamourous Rock epidemic. They're worse than shambling werewolves.

He told me to sit on my settee and not move. Said he would bring someone to be with me for safety and take down further information. Off he went, and came back a minute later, with WPC Crouch and her orange lipstick. Turns out they'd been working 'the case' together. I could tell that the relationship focused on other things, rather than apprehending criminals. I wished I'd put on my Biba velvet mini dress and taken my rollers out. I'd have given her a run for her money… as my brother would say.

So, he went into my garage to get a crowbar.

WPC Crouch leaned towards me on my floral Ercol settee. She complimented me on my taste in furniture and said nicely that she'd like to hear what happened from me. I started to explain about my neighbours being in a perpetual state of redecorating, but she waved me to silence. No, she meant how I'd killed my husband.

I stared at her orange coloured nails and wondered if they should match her lipstick.

'I've already told you who killed my husband,' I said.

This caused a somewhat heated debate, during which I informed her that the police knew George's murderer, and the Browns had poisoned the neighbours against me. I lost my temper, slightly. The problem is when awful things happen, people make assumptions based on little or no knowledge.

I heard Annette talking to Mrs Martin just this morning. She lives next door but one. Annette asked her what happened to Jean, and she said she didn't know. She said one day she was here and the next she wasn't. They'd had to get a skip to clear out her stuff. The last thing Jean was seen to have done? Come around to see me.

She didn't seem to get what I was saying and went off on a tangent.

'What did you talk about with Jean Anderson? Did she say something that upset you?'

I mean, was this woman there?

It was disturbing. Jean was like a mother to me. We'd always been honest with each other.

'Are they behind the wall, Hannah?' she asked me. She was looking through the kitchen door. Distracted.

'The Browns are behind that wall.' It was obvious, wasn't it? They were probably against it with a glass, hoping to catch snatches of our conversation.

I hated them at that moment. Horrible people.

'No, I meant Jean, and your husband?'

That made me angry.

Time to put things straight.

I went into the police station, and I told them it was Mr Watson in Accounts that had killed my George. They gave me a cup of tea, then told me to go home and take one of the tablets the doctor had given me.

They didn't listen. Like WPC Crouch.

William Watson Intermediate Accountant, champion javelin thrower at Bishop's Itchington Grammar School in 1952, with an appetite for success that outreached his aim. They had overlooked him in the company's search for a replacement to the indomitable Mr Tammin, who had left suddenly. He had sent a letter to the Deputy Director stating he was embarking on an expedition to the ancient tombs of Naghsh-e Rostam. George said Mr Tammin had never expressed a desire to visit locations on the Silk Road before. His usual holidays were to the Grand Hotel in Scarborough.

So, they promoted my George to Senior Accountant, and as a celebration he took himself off on the train to Harrogate. He got the bus to Barden and went walking on our favourite route alongside the river.

Jealousy is an ugly companion; almost as unpleasant as the passion of grief. Mr Watson followed my husband on his journey, right up to the foaming water. I wasn't there, but I have seen it in my mind every day, since I found out. He confessed to it much later; but it was a slip he made, at my husband's funeral, about the location of the accident. That was when I realised that George had been murdered, and his friend was the malefactor.

Admittedly, I resorted to dastardly measures to catch the killer. The Biba dress had an outing. Any hopes Mr Watson had of anything other than his just desserts were significantly bashed out of him that evening.

My only regret is that when I put him behind that wall, I left the trowel in the gap. It did give me some satisfaction to hear him desperately scratching near the end.

It was a good job I'd tied him up tight when he went in. I don't know how he lasted so long. Perhaps there was a leaky pipe he drank from. Apparently, you can live for months without food. I don't know. I'm quite partial to teacake at eleven.

He'd whisper at night, when I got myself settled with a good book and a cup of cocoa. It was mainly tedious information about his life, but he owned up to finishing off Mr Tammin, and Mr Akkerman from Catering (he stumbled on a piece of Mr Tammin in the mix for Wednesday's cottage pie in the canteen kitchen). He also said the accident involving Mabel Maughan the switchboard operator and the Welsh dresser in the canteen was orchestrated by himself. She became suspicious after Mr Akkerman had not arrived in the ladies' powder room as previously arranged, and going to investigate, discovered the Intermediate Accountant adding large portions of the Catering Manager into the sausage maker.

I got fed up with it in the end. I couldn't hear Brian Ford on the radio. I must admit I was disappointed when they stopped the science on Kaleidoscope earlier this year. But that's another story.

The thing is, most of the deaths at the steelworks can be credited to Mr Watson—apart from the Director, Mr Washbourne. He fell off the roof of his house unaided. So, the mystery of how he got himself up there in the first place remains unsolved.

And Mr Watson came to realise that his one act of violence had set him on an awful path of concealment that finished with him trussed up in my old washing line, behind the wall.

I didn't tell WPC Crouch any of this. She wasn't listening by this time. Perhaps I hit her too hard with the coal scuttle. A head wound bleeds rather a lot.

I hope she was conscious when I spoke about Jean.

The last time I saw her, Jean told me she was going away with a man she'd met on a Wallace Arnold Coach tour to Devon.

It upset me. I loved Jean.

Sometimes you have to let go of people, painful as it is.

I have cried an awful lot the past few minutes. Not just about losing Jean, George, and now PC Bramham. Such is my lot, I have yet another burden, which I will explain.

I don't want to leave without cleaning up the mess.

WPC Crouch is locked in the outside toilet.

PC Bramham is also fettered. We were burgled a few weeks before George went on his last walk. They took his tools, so he constructed a bit of a mantrap in the garage. Nothing awful. Just an inability to open the door once you are inside.

My husband had to come and rescue me a few times, when I'd gone in to get a hammer or my dead fly pot.

So, I considered my deeds and realised that the only dead body was the one in the wall. I took the hammer and the crowbar (I keep them in the pantry now, so I don't die of starvation in the garage) and knocked a hole in the wall.

My plan was to take the body of Mr Watson out in my old chintz curtains to the camper van I bought with George's insurance money. I would have to dispose of it somewhere between here and the ferry at Dover. I thought perhaps a ditch, or in some spinney. Gangsters bury their bodies in shallow graves in woods.

Imagine my surprise when he fell out on me and asked for a cup of tea.

Now I have a dusty, desperate looking man demanding more teacake. It does need eating, but now my plans have changed.

I'll take him with me. My mother used to say it was better to keep an eye on the people who want to murder you.

Mr Watson denies such thoughts, but if I leave him here, he'd only say he was the latest victim of the steelworks' killer, and I'd be in more trouble than I already am.

I must go now.

I have loaded some of my mother's boxes into the camper, along with the spare washing line, and coal scuttle, in case the situation changes before we reach the ferry.

I am posting the manuscript on the way. I hope they accept it. It would make a change from the usual murder mysteries they sell in W H Smith.

Hannah Miller   October 1974

Glossary
(In the order of their appearance)

<u>Elizabeth</u>

Seamstress

One who earns a living by sewing. She has a sharp eye and ability to create beautiful things. Wasted on underwear. Nobody looks at that.

Midwife

Of old, the midwife was a brewer of mead. She also removed obstructions from a woman's body. And delivered babies.

Resurrectionist

Body snatcher of the recently deceased, they stole to supply medical students in the early Victorian era. Some would despatch to order.

Foundling

A poor orphan or a child that has been abandoned by its parents and found by another. These could also be of other species, for example faerie child. But I take this too far. That's another story.

Leech collector   A person who stood in bogs or marshes in the summer and collects leeches on their legs, then sold them on to the medical profession for bloodletting. An easier way to keep one's blood pressure low.

Perrier water   My mother was a lover of mineral water, and her use of the trademarked item is a mistake. Perrier water came into existence in 1898. It would have been called Table Water earlier in the century. Not as desirable. Poor Elizabeth. It was probably drawn from the well in the courtyard.

Laudanum   A tincture of morphine readily available in pharmacists for pain control and just about any other ailment the Victorians suffered with. It was cheaper than wine or gin.

Strychnine   A murderer's first choice for subtle despatches, although the victim would argue that it is a most horrible way to die. It's a shame I didn't have any in when I entertained Mr Watson.

Miss Johnson

Demon   Whilst Miss Johnson's are biblical, real demons spit in the street, gossip over the back fence, and scratch at walls.

Wolf   Not an ordinary canis lupus. A lycanthrope in this case. They are stronger and more difficult to kill than a werewolf. Which makes us wonder, is Mr Wentworth dead at the bottom of the ravine? That was the problem with my mother. Always inventing impossible situations.

Barghest   Contrary to my interruptions, I do like dogs. Even big black ones. There are various Black Dogs in Yorkshire. Some are portents of doom, and others bring immediate death. I have been told that the original landlord of the Legless Barghest accidentally knocked his pain relief medication into the vat of beer during a Wedding celebration. When the fuddled drinkers refused to leave, he brought out his black Labrador, which was mistaken in the confusion of alcohol and opiates, for the monstrous dog of the legend. The villagers dissipated loudly into the night. Some were found the next morning fifteen miles away, still under the influence. No-one in this instance was turned to stone or died as a direct result. Although a week later, the bride ran off with the postman, and the groom set fire to the posthouse, inadvertently burning a huge quantity of bonds that the groom himself had purchased and were due to be delivered to him that morning.

Gargoyle   Designed to ward off evil and divert rainwater, my mother developed quite an obsession with them. I'm sure they will surface in later stories. Not to be confused with a grotesque which is mere ornament and does not awake at night to fight the street spitters and wall scratchers.

Deacon Brodie   William Brodie was a cabinet maker and lock smith who got above himself. His evil-doing stemmed from gambling. The story goes that he built the first gallows in Edinburgh and was the first to use it.

Angel Gabriel   My mother used to talk about the Dark Angel. She had seen the picture of Gabriel, hiding his light under dark raiments. She had some interesting discussions about it with the local vicar at my aunt's Tupperware parties. Aunt Lucy finally relented on my mother's exile from her house in 1969. I think it had something to do with my aunt being completely deaf and misunderstanding a question my brother put to her.

Arcadia   Utopia. A vision of living in harmony with nature. In Greek mythology (according to my mother), this is where Pan lived. It must have been an unreal realm for the poor Victorians, living in their squalid tenements, battling disease. How they would have wished for the green pastures and flower-laden cottages that sprang from the imaginations of the artists of the time.

The Last Wolf

Pokeberries

Originating from America, the Indian Ink Plant is a weedy looking thing, but likely to grow in a shady forest, if it wishes. It removes impurities from both ends. My mother mistook it for something else when we were younger, and we all lost weight after our bilberry jam did more than improve our night vision.

Lime

Powdered lime has been a most useful mineral over the course of time. Only the Celts could take an Ancient Roman ingredient of concrete and dye their skin and hair with it. An example of this can be seen in the Louvre, with the magnificent statue of the Wounded Gaul. My mother stood for a long time staring at it when she took myself and my brother. I don't think she was admiring just the tousled hair. They did battle only wearing their arms.

Back to lime. It was less caustic in water. I imagine it would have made a very effective lice and mite eradicator. Perfect to dunk a little boy into. Poor Tommy. They forgot to add the water.

The entrails   If you haven't already guessed, these were the unfortunate remains of Mr Spindle.

Tanning   Artisans such as Mr Wentworth worked the skins to get them more pliable. Don't ask me the intricacies because I don't know. I remember at school my History teacher Miss Mumble telling us that women used to chew on the skin to soften it. It was John Tattersfield who told me, on the way home, that they used urine as well. I threw my shoes in the bin that night.

But the tanning process was not kind to the body, and sores developed, particularly on the lower legs, which would be in vats of – well, you know some of the ingredients. Thus Mr Wentworth's ulcers.

Poor Mr Wentworth. I am starting to feel quite sorry for him.

Bone-grubber   A rag and bone man. But not with a horse and cart as we know. Down on his luck, he would have searched the streets for bones and scraps to sell on, eating out of dustbins.

Thank you, for reading this. My mother may not have approved, but I think it's time the truth was made public. Winter is such a difficult month, but after comes the Spring. Growth and awakenings…

If you liked this book, I would be most grateful if you left a review.

If you are intrigued as to what comes next, go to the author's Wordpress site for the continuing story of Hannah Miller and her family.

lifebetterlead.wordpress.com

You can connect with the author from there.

TALES OF THE BOY IN WINTER

Printed in Poland
by Amazon Fulfillment
Poland Sp. z o.o., Wrocław

54991472R00047